I'm Going to Tell

NADINE GIBSON-ANDERSON

AuthorHouse™
1663 Liberty Drive
Bloomington, IN 47403
www.authorhouse.com
Phone: 1 (800) 839-8640

Because of the dynamic nature of the Internet, any web addresses or links contained in
this book may have changed since publication and may no longer be valid. The views
expressed in this work are solely those of the author and do not necessarily reflect the views
of the publisher, and the publisher hereby disclaims any responsibility for them.

Any people depicted in stock imagery provided by Getty Images are models,
and such images are being used for illustrative purposes only.
Certain stock imagery © Getty Images.

This book is printed on acid-free paper.

ISBN: 978-1-7283-5822-2 (sc)
ISBN: 978-1-7283-5821-5 (e)

Library of Congress Control Number: 2020906209

Print information available on the last page.

Published by AuthorHouse 04/22/2020

authorHOUSE®

I'm Going to Tell

NADINE GIBSON-ANDERSON

I would like to thank Samantha Dacosta for all her help towards making this book come to life.

I also want to thank my husband Dwayne Anderson for his encouragement as I worked on my book.

And last but not least my children Alexus Gibson and Malachi Hemmings for believing in their mom.

Jodi is an 8 year old girl who lives with her mother and her sister Faith. Faith is 3 years older than Jodi and is her best friend in the whole wide world.

Jodi is a very quiet and soft-spoken little girl unlike her sister Faith who is very outspoken, feisty and doesn't hold anything back.

Jodi loves going to the park to play with the other children where she can go on the swing, the slides and even play in the sprinklers. She also likes watching tv and spending time with her family.

Jodi's mom does her best to protect her daughters and is careful about who she leaves them with as well as where she leaves them. But one day Jodi's mom had to go away for a while to another country for work and had to leave her daughters in the care of trusted family members. Even though it was hard for her to leave her daughters behind she didn't have any other choice.

Jodi and Faith were very heartbroken that their mom had to leave them in the care of others because they had never spent any time apart from their mother before.

When the girls' mom dropped them off, they both had a sad look on their faces because they knew they would not see their mom for a long time. Their mom kissed them on their foreheads and hugged them so tight that they cried out, "Mom, we can't breathe" and she giggled to herself.

As they went inside the house with tears running down their cheeks they looked through the window and waved goodbye to their mom as the door closed behind them.

While they were at their cousin's house they were not happy because they were not able to go play with their friends or go to the park. They missed the swing, the slides and playing in the sprinklers.

Their mom would call every day and they were so excited to hear her voice over the phone. Each time they spoke to her they would ask her the same questions, "Mommy, when are you coming to get us and when are we going home?" Their mom answered and said, "Very soon my precious daughters! Mommy loves you both very much ok."

One day, Faith noticed that Jodi wasn't as playful as she used to be. She had this sad look on her face and her head was always hanging down.

Faith called out to her, "Jodi, what's wrong? Mom always teaches us not to keep secrets." Jodi then held her head up and said, "Nothing, I'm ok" but Faith knew she was telling a fib, she knew something was wrong with Jodi.

Faith kept pressing her sister to tell her why she was so unhappy. "You can tell me anything Jodi!" said Faith.

With tears in her eyes Jodi yelled, "I have something to tell you but I'm scared!" Faith replied, "Don't be afraid little sis, I am here for you and you can tell me anything." The words were so hard for Jodi to say yet she couldn't help but blurt it out as loud as she could, "Cousin Mike would come in my room at night and touch my special place. Mommy said no one is supposed to touch our special place and we aren't supposed to touch theirs! Mommy always teaches us that if anyone ever touches our special place we should tell her and if she's not around to tell someone else. And to never keep it as a secret because some secrets can destroy you."

Mommy always taught her girls that even if the person who touched your special place told you that they would hurt you, you should still tell somebody and if that person doesn't believe you find someone else that will. And never keep it a secret.

"He told me not to tell anyone and that he will buy me toys, take me to the store and buy me whatever I want," said Jodi.

One day while the girls were playing in the backyard, a lady walked up behind them out of nowhere. They turned around and were very surprised to see who it was "Mommy! Mommy!" shouted both girls.

They ran and jumped in her arms. With tears running down their cheeks they hugged for what seemed like forever. The girls began to tell their mom about cousin Mike touching Jodi in her special place. Mom had a concerned look on her face but she said, "You're so brave for telling me and I'm so proud of you." The girls were so happy that their mom was there; they knew she came to take them home. Both girls were so relieved to be leaving that horrible, horrible house of nightmares and to know that their mom would never send them back there ever again.

A PRAYER FOR OUR CHILDREN

Suffer the little children to come unto him and forbid them not for theirs is the kingdom of Heaven. Lord Jesus, please watch over our children. Protect them from the predators and those who will abuse and mistreat them! Please keep them as the apple of your eye and be a force shield all around them in Jesus' name I pray, amen and amen.

NOTE TO PARENTS

Look for signs that your child / children might give as they may not always seem like signs.

- Changes in behavior around people they were normally friendly and/or comfortable around
- Listen when a child / children say that they're being touched
- Changes in behavior like becoming withdrawn, outbursts of anger and even being sad a lot
- Unusual behavior during bath time (Ex: not wanting to take off their clothes)

**THESE MAY NOT BE THE ONLY SIGNS
BE VIGILANT TO CHANGES IN YOUR
CHILD / CHILDREN AND NEVER BE
AFRAID TO ASK AND TO LISTEN**

Printed in the United States
By Bookmasters